Eric Carle is the creator of more than seventy picture books for young readers.

Eric Carle was born in Syracuse, New York. However, when he was just six, he moved with his parents to Germany. In 1952, after graduating from the prestigious *Akademie der Bildenden Künste* in Stuttgart, he fulfilled his dream of returning to New York.

Eric Carle has received many distinguished awards and honors for his work, including, in 2003, the Laura Ingalls Wilder Award for his lifetime contribution to children's literature and illustration.

In 2002, fifty years after Carle's return to the United States, *The Eric Carle Museum of Picture Book Art* was opened in Amherst, Massachusetts. Here visitors of all ages can enjoy, in addition to Eric Carle's work, original artwork by other distinguished children's book illustrators from this country and abroad.

Photograph by Motoko Inoue

July 2003

RUBBER DUCKS LOST AT SEA

In 1992, a shipment of 29,000 rubber bathtub toys, including ducks, beavers, turtles and frogs, fell overboard from a container ship.

Some of these rubber toys have washed up on the shores of Alaska, while others have made their way through the Bering Strait, past icebergs, around the northern coast of Greenland and into the Atlantic Ocean.

Many of these toys ing found along the and they are att people f

towns to
collecti
Ducks
to the
moor
ort
M
e

I could not resist making a story out of this newspaper report.
I hope you like my story. *Eric Carle*

For Toby Cole

Ann Beneduce, Creative Editor

10 Little Rubber Ducks
Copyright © 2005 by Eric Carle
Sound design by Wesley Talbot
Manufactured in China
All rights reserved.
www.harperchildrens.com
www.eric-carle.com
Library of Congress Cataloging-in-Publication Data
Carle, Eric.
10 little rubber ducks / by Eric Carle.— 1st ed.
    p.   cm.
Summary: When a storm strikes a cargo ship, ten rubber ducks are tossed
overboard and swept off in ten different directions. Based on a factual incident.
ISBN 0-06-074075-2
[1. Toys—Fiction. 2. Ducks—Fiction.] I. Title: Ten little rubber ducks. II. Title.
PZ7.C21476Aah 2005
[E]—dc22   2004001420
                                                    CIP
                                                    AC

1 2 3 4 5 6 7 8 9 10
❖
First Edition

10 Little Rubber Ducks

Eric Carle

HarperCollins*Publishers*

Chuckedy–chuckedy–chuck
goes the rubber duck machine.
Out pop little yellow rubber ducks
one after the other,

one after the other.

The little rubber ducks are painted—bills red and eyes blue.

Then they are packed, 10 to a box...

and off they go...

to be loaded onto a cargo ship.

"Hello," calls the captain.

The captain and his cargo ship
are taking the little rubber ducks
across the wide sea to faraway countries,

                              to faraway countries.

Suddenly a storm churns the water into big waves.
A strong wind whistles across the sea,
                        whistles across the sea.

A big wave lifts up one of the boxes
and throws it into the water.
The box opens, and 10 little rubber ducks fall out.
"10 rubber ducks overboard!" shouts the captain.

"10 rubber ducks overboard!"

After some time the storm calms down.
The 10 little rubber ducks bob in the big wide sea.
As far as one can see—only water and sky,

water and sky.

The 10 little rubber ducks begin to drift apart.

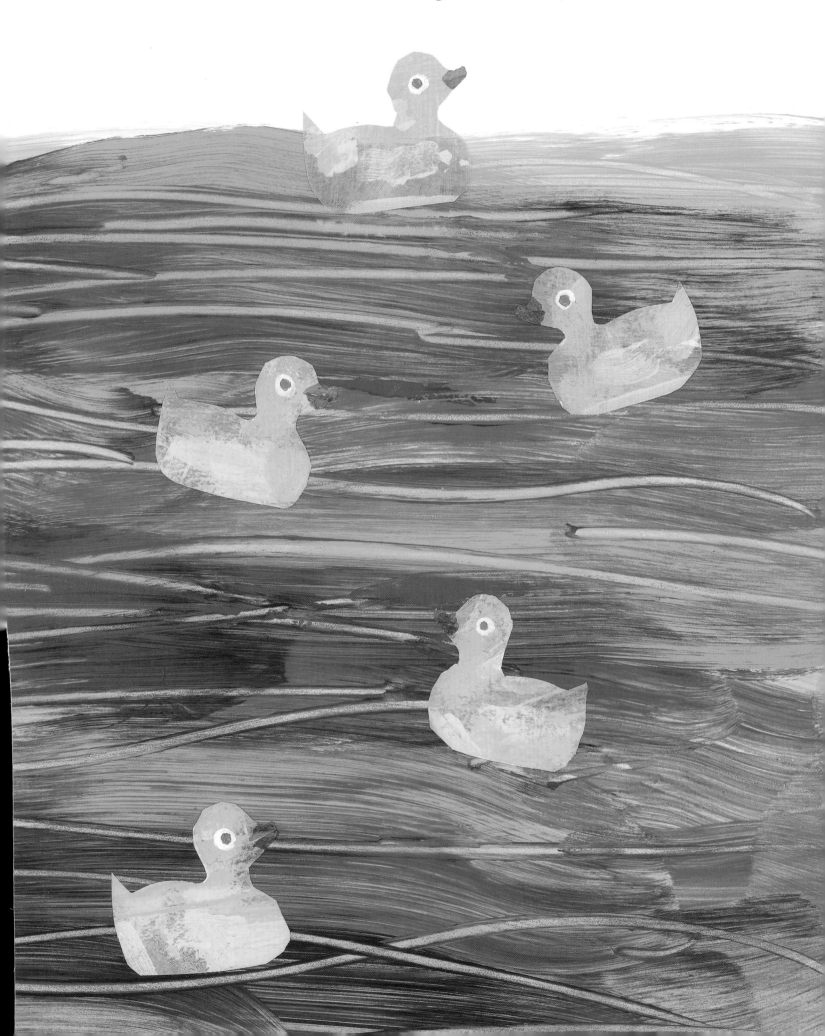

The 1st little rubber duck drifts west.
A dolphin jumps over it.

The **2nd** little rubber duck drifts east.
A seal barks at it.

The **3rd** little rubber duck drifts north.
A polar bear growls at it.

The **4th** little rubber duck drifts south.
A flamingo stares at it.

The **5**th little rubber duck drifts to the left.
A pelican chatters at it.

The **6**th little rubber duck drifts to the right.
A turtle glides past it.

The **7**th little rubber duck drifts up.
An octopus blinks at it.

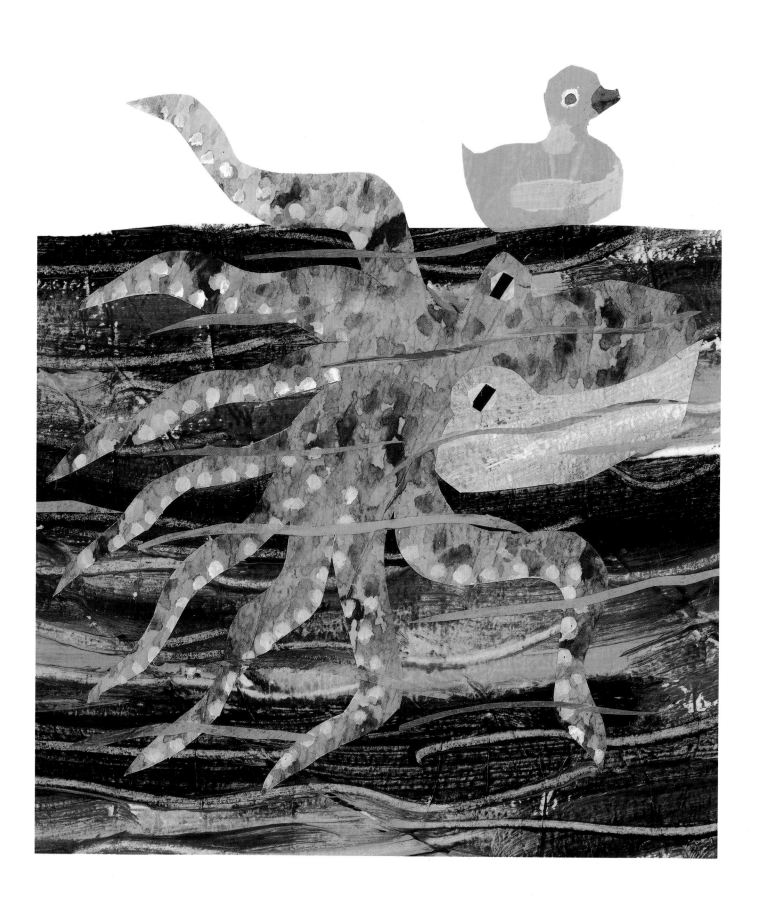

The **8**th little rubber duck drifts down.
A seagull screeches at it.

The **9**th little rubber duck drifts this way.
A whale sings to it.

The **10**th little rubber duck drifts that way,
bobbing and floating on the big wide sea.
The sun is setting. It is getting dark.

As far as one can see—only water and sky,

water and sky.

The next morning the 10th little rubber duck
meets a mother duck and her ducklings.
"Quack!" says the mother duck.

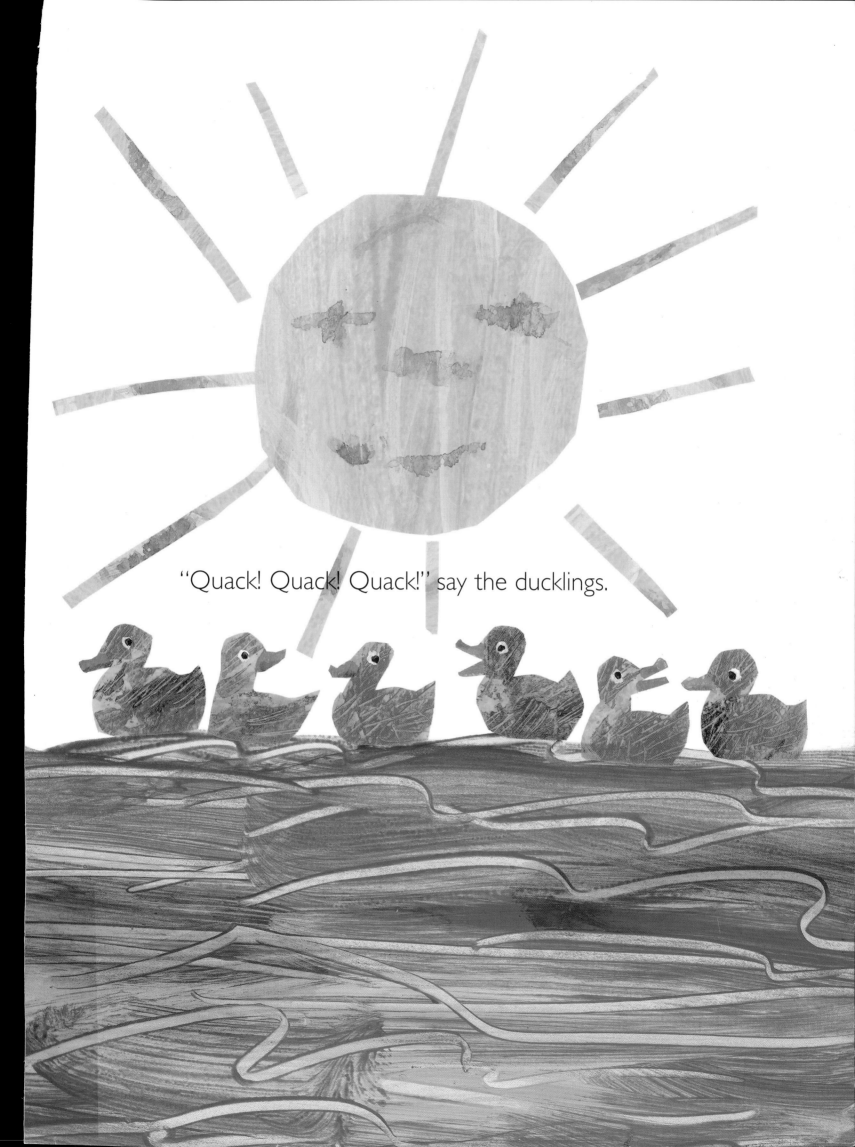

"Quack! Quack! Quack!" say the ducklings.

At the end of the day, the sun sets again.
It is getting dark. The mother duck and
her ducklings swim toward their nest.

The little rubber duck floats along with them.

"Good Night!" says the moon.
"Quack!" says the mother duck.
"Quack! Quack! Quack!" say the ducklings.

press here

"Squeak!" says the little rubber duck.